DO YOU KNOW GOD LOVES YOU?

YES, it is True!

Written by: Jovan Gomez

Illustrated by: Wendy McCarthy

XULON PRESS

Xulon Press
2301 Lucien Way #415
Maitland, FL 32751
407.339.4217
www.xulonpress.com

Unless otherwise indicated, Scripture quotations taken from (Version(s) used)

Printed in the United States of America.

Paperback ISBN-13: 9781662800443
Ebook ISBN-13: 9781662800450

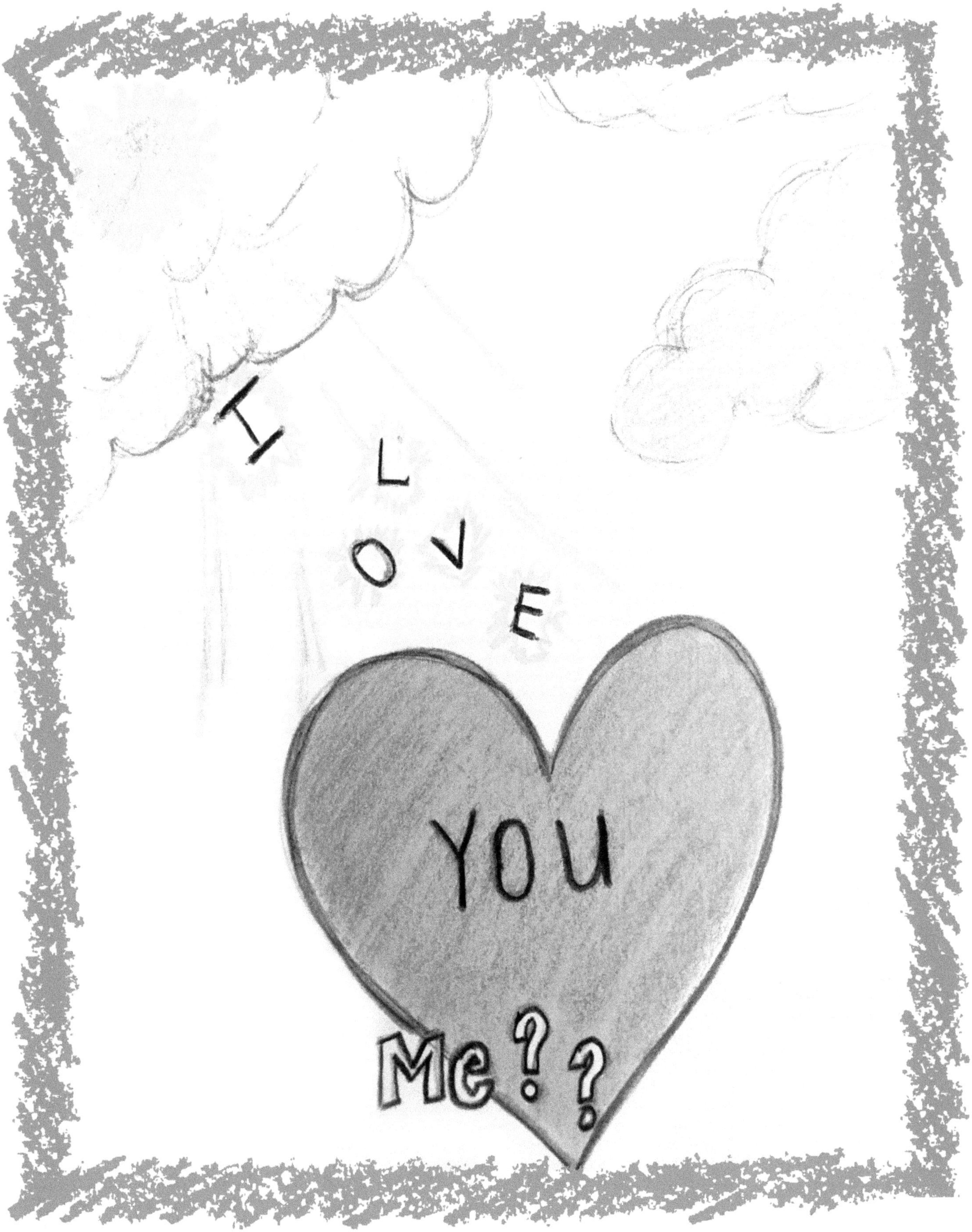
I LOVE
YOU
Me??

He loves you
from your head to your toes.
You may wonder how I know.
Well! My friend the Bible
tells me so.

He loves you
when you're mad,
when you're sad,
he even loves you when
you've been bad.

mad

sad

happy

been bad

And if you're sorry...
God will forgive and
teach you how to live!

In the beginning, God created EVERYTHING!

He made the
sun shine bright,
made the moon and stars
to light up your night.

With his hands,
he made these lands.
He made the birds, the bees,
all the animals, the air
and trees.

He
did
this
all
for
YOU.

He did this all
because
He loves you!

With his breath,
we came to be.
He did this all,
can't you see?

You're here for a reason,
let it be clear.

God loves you in EVERY season.
So, let's all cheer...

Hooray for God's love!

God's love is
a treasure we all hold
He loves you
and this you MUST know!